The Great Petrowski

Also by Gina Berriault

The Great petrowski

A FABLE

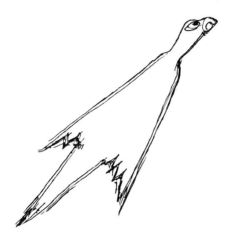

Story and illustrations by

Gina Berriault

COUNTERPOINT

WASHINGTON, D.C.

The first edition of this book was published in a limited edition by Thumbprint Press in Fairfax, California.

Library of Congress Cataloging-in-Publication Data
Berriault, Gina.
    The great Petrowksi / Gina Berriault.
        p. cm.
    ISBN 1-58243-074-8 (alk. paper)
    1. Parrots—Fiction. 2. Singers—Fiction. 3. Opera—Fiction. I. Title.
    PS3552.E738 G7 2000
    813'.54—dc21   99-087232

FIRST PRINTING

Jacket and text design by Amy Evans McClure
Printed in Canada

COUNTERPOINT
P.O. Box 65793
Washington, D.C. 20035-5793

Counterpoint is a member of the Perseus Books Group

10 9 8 7 6 5 4 3 2 1

For Julie Elena, again

Illustrations

The Great Petrowski

A LONE PARROT FLEW about the city every day. This was a city in North America and a parrot on the wing was a strange sight. He perched at the top of the tallest towers where he was able to see all around even while resting. Since he did this over and over he probably had not yet found what he was looking for. He was seen strutting through rain puddles on the flat roofs, safer up there than in the streets where the rain flowed into gutters. The city dwellers set out cups and bowls of sunflower seeds on window sills. He kept his distance. At night he slept on the highest branch in the largest, leafiest tree in the public park. Then one evening, strollers in the park waited in vain for the sight of him settling in for the night.

Flying home late, way after sunset, the parrot was deep in thought and this made him feel heavier. He had spent the day in search of a grove of rainswept jungle trees that he remembered but never found. All other birds seemed to give no thought at all to where on earth they first saw the light of day, finding it pleasant enough just where they were. But often in the night, in dreams, he heard again the sounds of another place and felt his feathers stirred by other airs.

That night was the first night of the opera season. The opera house was ablaze with lights, and colored banners floated on the evening winds. Throngs of people were coming from all directions. The parrot, already flying incautiously low, flapped down lower to see what was going on. A woman screamed when he came too close and the man beside her struck at his tail. Thrown off balance, the parrot went skimming crazily over the crowd, dragging a long silk scarf from a

The opera house was ablaze with lights

woman's curls and dropping it on a man's hat. Alarmed, lost, he flew into the open door of the opera house, scattering tickets and programs.

Up toward the ceiling he flew and around the chandeliers that he mistook for trees glittering with rain and moonlight. Persons on their way to their red plush seats stopped to look up at him, causing consternation in the aisles. Several of his feathers were drifting around on all the warm breaths rising.

At last he perched on the center chandelier, just in time before everything went dark. In a large pit before the stage, tiny lamps lit up. The orchestra down there began to play. Musical instruments flashed and glowed, hands flew over strings and keys, heads bobbed. All this activity was bringing forth amazing sounds from another time and place the parrot had almost forgotten. Skyward sounds and deep underground sounds of roots moving, sounds of stealthy winds and of an immense forest thrashing about, of heavy rains, and the voices of animals and birds.

Like clouds, a golden curtain rose and beyond it a silver curtain parted. On the stage a

The orchestra began to play

woman in a long ruffled dress, like feathers, and a man in a coat like a raven's wings began to sing. Their voices glided up and dipped down, flew away into silence and instantly swooped back. Their voices coiled around the parrot's chandelier and rustled around in his feathers. The clouds closed up and parted again many times, and a different scene was revealed each time. A park with delicate trees came and went before the parrot could make up his mind to escape

♪

into that pale blue sky. A cathedral came and went. And more singers sang.

Thunder! The audience was standing up, clapping hands and shouting. Alarmed, the parrot flew off his perch and around the ceiling again. Were they trying to scare him away? But no one was looking up at him. The people below were throwing flowers at the singers, who were now bowing to the audience. Then the parrot understood. The clapping people were like birds, flapping their wings and calling out to those they wished to mate with. And he settled again on his perch.

NOW THE OPERA HOUSE was empty and silent. The parrot opened his beak to sing everything he had heard that night. Only familiar sounds came out. Quacks of ducks on the pond in the park, barks of dogs, yells of boys, roars of trucks, screeches of autos, shouts of children, cries of infants, and laughter of all sorts. When at last a soprano attempted to be heard, a crow's warning cut her short.

The Janitor held up a cookie, hoping to coax the parrot down. Intent on his garbled repertoire, the parrot took no notice.

Night after night, the parrot basked in all the voices singing of love and longing, of rage and revenge, of sorrow and loss, of hope and fate and love again. There was such a profusion of marvelous sounds and sights, the parrot was dizzied by it all. And night after night, when everyone was gone and only a dim light burned on the stage, he flew down, ate the sunflower seeds, the crackers, the apple slices left for him by the Janitor, and drank the clear water in a lake-blue bowl. Then he ran through the night's opera. The more he sang, the fewer were the barks and yawks, and the more pleased he was with himself.

One night, Mr. Alonzo, the Opera Director, was on his way home when he discovered he had lost his gold and ruby ring. On the instant he swung a U-turn and drove back to the opera house. The ring, given to him by a famous soprano as a memento of a sweet season of love, was too large and tended to slip off his finger when people who came backstage shook his hand too vigorously. He had been plump at the time of the gift but had lost weight as a result of heartbreak.

Mr. Alonzo was just beginning to search the dressing rooms when he heard someone singing. A soprano was singing, soon joined by a tenor. Then a baritone chimed in. By now, the cast ought to be fast asleep elsewhere. Mr. Alonzo peered around the curtain. No one was out there in the whole empty opera house. Only a parrot was there, strutting close to the unlit footlights, singing.

Mr. Alonzo crept down into a second row seat, where he hoped he would not be seen. Flinging wide an imaginary cloak, the parrot climbed the curtain to an imaginary balcony and, clinging there, sang of love. Gently fluffing out a wing, the parrot became the soprano, answering her beloved. Tears ran down Mr. Alonzo's cheeks, so moved was he by the several miraculous voices coming from one parrot.

When the last aria was over, Mr. Alonzo sprang to his feet, clapping and shouting, "Bravo! Bravo!"

Shocked, the parrot flew halfway up to his chandelier, changed his mind in mid-air, and flew back down to take a bow. He took several

9

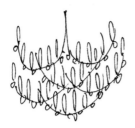

Only a parrot was there

bows, until caution overcame him and he flew back up to his perch.

"I'd like very much to make an appointment with you," Mr. Alonzo called up. "Whenever you can spare the time." He bowed to the parrot and graciously bade him goodnight.

The next night, when the audience and cast and crew were gone, Mr. Alonzo and the Janitor took seats in the front row. A Young Soprano stepped out on the stage and sang to the parrot up on his chandelier. Perfectly on time, the parrot joined her in the duet, singing the tenor role. When the duet was over, she bowed to the audience. Then, after hesitating only a moment, the parrot flew down and bowed beside her, close to her green satin shoes.

Four gilded chairs and a small table were brought out onto the stage. Poppy seed cakes, sesame seed crackers, fruit tarts, plums, grapes, and mineral water in green bottles were set out on the white tablecloth. Then they all sat down around the table to celebrate the discovery of this miracle of a parrot.

Introductions were made, but when the parrot's turn came he found he had no name. All agreed a name must be found.

"Parotti?" suggested the Soprano.

"Perushki?" suggested the Janitor.

"Figaro?" The parrot offered.

"Petrowski," said Mr. Alonzo.

Solemnly, the parrot repeated that name. Then he nodded his acceptance.

The next night, perched on Mr. Alonzo's shoulder, Petrowski was introduced to the Singers as they were putting on their costumes. At their request he sang some very difficult passages and everyone was amazed.

"They praise you to the skies," said Mr. Alonzo. "And that is only appropriate, since you came to us from the skies."

The Baritone, whose deep voice shook the ruff around his neck as he spoke, asked Petrowski: "How can a bird with such a small chest bring forth a voice so powerful?"

"Petrowski sings from the heart, that's how," said the Young Soprano.

"My guess," said Mr. Alonzo to Petrowski, "is that you spent your early youth soaring on the world's purest air. Other great singers can only imagine that experience. Can you tell us where you were born?"

"Hatched, you mean," said the Baritone.

"Same thing," said Mr. Alonzo.

"Singing," said Petrowski, "is waking memories, but I may not ever know the place where I was born until I find myself there again."

A FEW NIGHTS LATER Mr. Alonzo was in a terrible state and the cast was in an uproar. The renowned tenor who was to sing that night had fallen ill and the tenor who was always waiting around to take his place in just such an emergency was nowhere to be found. Mr. Alonzo ran around witlessly, loudly recalling other disasters of his career. Petrowski, on his shoulder, had a rough ride. At five minutes to curtain time, Mr. Alonzo paused before a mirror to smooth down his feathery white hair, adjust his tie, and calm himself. The moment had come for him to step out from behind the

Hope spread its wings in the Opera Director's heart

golden curtain and inform the audience that the night's performance was cancelled.

Petrowski had never before viewed himself in a mirror. He took this opportunity to observe both sides of his profile, the shimmer of his feathers in the light from the many little globes around the mirror, and the composure and grace that, up to this moment, he had no idea he possessed. Mr. Alonzo also gazed at Petrowski and hope spread its wings in the Opera Director's heart.

With Petrowski flying just above his head, Mr. Alonzo ran to the Wardrobe Mistress and the Seamstress, who were always ready to pin up a dragging hem or sew up a split sleeve. At once the Seamstress stitched a velvet cloak for Petrowski, and the Wardrobe Mistress nimbly put together a broadbrim hat with a long plume.

As the curtain began to rise, Mr. Alonzo hissed into Petrowski's ear. "Please, I beg of you. Sing only the tenor and nobody else."

Petrowski sang gloriously. The very necessity to sing only one role brought out the high passion of his tenor voice. When the role called for

He flew to the top of the proscenium
arch above the stage

him to embrace the Young Soprano, he managed this by flying up to her hand, which she held as a perch over her heart, and spreading his wings across her bosom. The applause was thunderous. So many flowers were thrown to him, the pile hid him from view. A flower in his beak, he flew to the top of the proscenium arch above the stage and made his bows up there.

OVERNIGHT, PETROWSKI BECAME a celebrity. With Mr. Alonzo and with a valet, Oliver, who saw that his capes were brushed free of clinging crumbs and seeds, he flew by jet plane to New York City. There he sang in that city's famed opera house and received a standing ovation. Critics called his voice, or voices, magnificent, incomparable, incredible. An impresario offered a private jet and they flew across the ocean to Europe. There, Prime Ministers and Presidents, Dignitaries of all sorts, Famous Musicians, and other Great Singers came to hear him and to meet him.

Love letters awaited him wherever he went

Since tickets cost a great deal in any language, the thousands who could not afford to hear him thronged the streets of the opera houses and concert halls, hoping just to catch a glimpse of him.

Love letters awaited him wherever he went. A Countess wrote that she lived alone in a mansion surrounded by vast orchards of delectable fruits. Could he visit? Petrowski replied that his engagement calendar denied him that pleasure.

A shopgirl wrote to tell him that she had spent her entire savings for a seat in the farthest row of the gallery and dreamed of how he would fly up there and carry her away with him. Petrowski was touched by the letter but could not oblige.

At last it was Beatrice who captivated Petrowski. A soprano, her voice was birdsweet and passionate, and she possessed her own lustrous reputation. A tiny woman of exquisite beauty,

At last it was Beatrice who captivated Petrowski

she wore colorful, floating garments, and her dark curls were held up by jeweled combs. They met in Milan, Italy, and in that city's opera house they sang together for the first time. Armloads of flowers were tossed upon the stage, fragrant flowering herbs were thrown, and even stalks of wheat.

Introduzzione
Trombe
Violini
Violini
THE GR. PETROWSKI
TONIGHT

OUTH AMERICA WAS THE continent Petrowski chose to tour next. It beckoned him, he told Mr. Alonzo. Beatrice happily agreed to accompany him. She brought along her niece and close companion, Lucia, who helped her in and out of her costumes and saw to it that she kept to her diet.

As the plane approached the shores of that continent, Petrowski confided to his companions that he was almost certain it was the place of his birth. He was remembering trees as high as city buildings, their tops an endless canopy, monkeys with golden manes, and cats much

He had escaped from a boat's black hold

larger and fiercer than any city cats, and pounding rains, and curling leaves that caught the rain for the birds and insects who never came down to the ground. Or all this might have been only a dream, he said, the night he slept alone in a harsh cypress tree at the edge of a cold, roaring ocean. He had escaped, he said, from a boat's black hold filled with captive birds, some of whom did not survive. When captured he was young, he said, and he hoped that he was now still young even after that timeless voyage.

The evening of their arrival in Brazil, Petrowski was the honored guest at a sumptuous party in the presidential palace. While Beatrice and Lucia danced with President Fado and Dignitaries, and Oliver, a very fine dancer, danced with their wives and daughters, and Mr. Alonzo observed all details, Petrowski sat with Estrella, the President's wife, in the music room.

She told him she had been a poor girl, singing in a little cabaret, when the gentleman who was to become President proposed marriage.

Together they sang the romantic songs she used to sing

"Like myself," she said, "you sang your way from obscurity to the heights."

They sat down at the grand piano, Petrowski on the lid. Together they sang the romantic songs she used to sing in the little cabaret.

After a spectacular performance in the opera house, Petrowski told President Fado that he now wished to explore the country's rainforest. The President offered his own private jet to enable Petrowski to fly over the rainforest in comfort. Petrowski gracefully refused the offer.

ABOARD A SLOW, ancient train, Petrowski and his companions entered the rainforest. Masses of trees towered over the little train, their tops so entangled that sunlight barely came through. Every once in a while the Engineer and the Conductor climbed down from the train and chopped away at the thick vines growing over the tracks.

Like Petrowski, Mr. Alonzo had wished to explore this famous jungle. In his long career as opera director he had cured many singers of stage fright, love loss, and other ailments affecting the throat. Take deep breaths, he

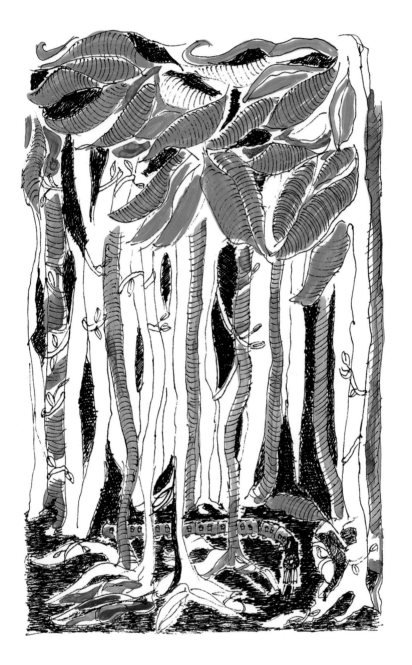

Masses of trees towered over the little train

advised them, and if possible, find some fresh air to do it in.

"The air! The air!" Mr. Alonzo now cried as the wheels clacked slowly on. "My friends, breathe more deeply than ever before in your lives! These trees are bringing forth the oxygen we require and here we are, right where it's happening. Every schoolchild knows all about it but no one is more grateful for this generous gift than singers."

"Not more grateful than we who listen," said Oliver.

A giant moth, heavenly mauve, drifted by their window, going faster than the train. And from all around the voices of the forest's inhabitants were heard, voices belonging to predators and prey and to any and all creatures from frog to feline.

"It's just as I remember it," said Petrowski.

A drenching rain began to fall. They banged shut their window and were almost shaken off their seats by the downpour. The rain stopped as suddenly as it had begun and they opened the window again. Water was dripping and sliding rapidly everywhere, making low vibrant sounds and high crystal sounds, deep twangs like a double-bass and even horn and drum sounds.

"The orchestra is tuning up!" cried Beatrice.

"Do you see what I see?" cried Mr. Alonzo, and he raised the binoculars to his eyes. "It's so deep in the trees, so far away, I can hardly make it out. It appears to be a very ancient and mouldering opera house, with only a trace of its former grandeur. What do you suppose it's doing here?"

At that moment, a cloud of smoke came swirling into their compartment.

"Close all windows!" the Conductor shouted. Carrying his broom, he came running down the aisle. "Close all windows!"

Up and down the train, windows were banged shut again. A child began to cry. The wet leaves and fern fronds and petals that were plastered on their windowpane by the rain now began to slip off in the dry air. Through the smoky glass they saw men slashing and sawing the trees, throwing branches and trunks into roaring fires. They heard the chainsaws rasping

and grinding, they heard the trees striking the ground, they heard the fires crackling and exploding. A terrible din.

"Are we in Hell?" cried Lucia. She always carried in her purse a small Bible in a gold-threaded velvet cover.

"Calm down, young lady!" said the Conductor. "It's just some poor farmless farmers out there, clearing away the trees so they can grow food for their families. Coffee plantations have taken over their little farms so that you, young lady, can have your hot cup of coffee every morning."

"I do not drink coffee," said Lucia. "Only tea, and once in a while a hot cup of cocoa."

"Then I beg your pardon," the Conductor said. "But every day this train hauls in more hungry families and every day we haul more families out again. The soil here won't grow anything but rainforest. You see this broom? I sweep up the ashes they leave behind in the aisle."

"Listen!" cried Petrowski.

"I am trying *not* to listen," cried Beatrice, pressing her hands over her ears.

34

"What would you say if I joined them?"

"Up above the noise. Can you hear it?" cried Petrowski.

"Not at all!" cried Beatrice.

"Then open the window!" cried Petrowski. "Never mind the smoke!"

Beatrice hung out the window, weeping

Oliver threw open the window again. Circling high above the din and the smoke, flocks of birds were making an awesome racket of their own. Screams of outrage, screeches of fear, shrieks of sorrow, threats.

"Parrots," said Petrowski. As if caught by a large python, he appeared to be struggling in the coils of a dilemma.

"What would you say if I joined them?" Petrowski asked his companions.

"But when will you return?" cried Beatrice.

"That, my dear, I cannot say."

The emotion heard in songs at parting was heard now in their voices.

Then Petrowski embraced Beatrice, nodded farewell to his dear companions, and flew to the open window. For a moment he was poised there, his feathers shaken by the hot winds from the fires. Then he was gone.

Leaning far out the window, Mr. Alonzo and Beatrice caught their last sight of him, his brilliant feathers flashing higher and higher in the smoke.

The train stopped. The passengers poured out, calling for Petrowski. Mr. Alonzo ventured out among the felled trees, shaking his silver-tipped cane at the figures in the smoke. Oliver and the Conductor restrained him and brought him back into the train. Beatrice hung out the window, weeping. The passengers, coughing, staggered back to their seats. For five minutes, and an extra two minutes more, the Engineer blasted the train whistle at full volume, a warning to Petrowski that he had only those minutes in which to change his mind. He did not return.

S INGERS EVERYWHERE dedicated their performances to Petrowski. Opera singers, pop singers, rock singers, blues singers, country and western singers, jazz singers, all told of his inspiring influence on their careers. An underestimated bird, he had overcome the odds against him and attained the pinnacle. Children began to

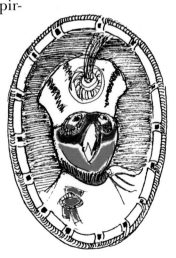

imagine that Petrowski was a magician, half-bird, half-human, who lived centuries ago and invented singing.

A YEAR PASSED. OVER THE northern hemisphere a record cold winter set in. Beatrice, worn out by her many performances on the stages of Europe and by her longing for Petrowski, came down with a severe sore throat. She cancelled further engagements. Bundled up in a heavy coat and a huge woolen muffler, she flew back to Brazil. She took the train to the little hotel where they had spent the night after Petrowski's farewell. Trees were still standing but not as many as a year ago.

At dawn she was wakened by many voices

singing. Wrapped in her kimono and woolen muffler, she stepped out. Up in the trees parrots were singing arias dear to her heart. Whether flying or perched or preening, they were singing. Although no voice was as marvelous as Petrowski's they could all be considered beautiful. Beatrice was overjoyed. She was given reason to hope that this day or the next, and a few steps farther into the forest, she would hear *his* voice soaring above the rest.

The Hotel Keeper, a man who resembled a thin brown beetle with black spots, asked Beatrice if Petrowski had sung in Portugal, in the city of Lisbon where he was born ninety years ago. He was delighted when she told him Yes. His two littlest children, a boy and a girl, whose mother was a Forest Indian, offered to be her guides. Alone, she might get lost.

They set out into the morning mists. Here and there they were forced to climb over felled trees and skirt around piles of charred tree limbs. The children told her what the Forest People believed about Petrowski, that he had

They set out into the morning mists

flown down from a higher realm and not from out the train window. They told her that in times of great crises, the Beings who lived in that realm came down to earth as animals and birds to see what they could do.

The deeper they went into the forest, a greater number of parrots were heard singing. But Petrowski's voice was not among them. That night Beatrice wrote to Mr. Alonzo.

My dear Mr. Alonzo,

Not yet! I have not yet heard or sighted our dear Petrowski. How strange it is to hear, all around in the forest, voices inspired by his own. You cannot imagine how many parrots are singing arias, and with what joy! A sad note is also heard, however. The more voices raised in song, the fewer trees there are for the singers to call their own. My dear friend, I have decided to stay on here in this forest as long as there is a forest, even until the last tree falls. The fervent hope that I may someday find our beloved Petrowski keeps me here.

Beatrice

Drawn by her lantern light, a considerable number of very large luminous moths of many colors throbbed and fluttered against the window screen, and she wondered if they were imploring her to save them and their forest home.

Backstage at the opera house in Geneva, Switzerland, Mr. Alonzo stood transfixed, reading Beatrice's letter. The letter had just been delivered to him by a messenger from the hotel where Mr. Alonzo and the cast were staying. It was two seconds before curtain time.

"Mr. Alonzo, we all wish to begin," the Baritone pleaded.

"Exactly," said Mr. Alonzo. "Begin, and sing as you have never sung before."

With the hand that held the letter, he signaled for the curtain to be raised. Then, waving the letter, he ran to the nearest phone, which was in his own office, backstage. It took an hour and twenty minutes, but at last his voice reached the ancient wall phone in the tiny lobby of the hotel deep in the Brazilian rainforest.

"I don't care what time it is there, day or night, or what season, wake her up!" he told the Hotel Keeper.

Beatrice was in her hammock bed, down with fever and chills and loneliness. She came to the phone. Even from so far away, Mr. Alonzo's voice carried more than its usual persuasion.

"How many parrots are singing?" he demanded.

"Oh, enough for a chorus," she said. "Or more."

"I know what he's up to!" Mr. Alonzo shouted. "Reserve all seats on that train!"

"Why must I bring a trainload," she cried. "Why not Petrowski alone?"

"Not Petrowski alone and certainly not without him. Now go and sing to him as you have never sung before. I promise you he will appear."

"I am hoarse," she said.

"When the moment comes you will not be," he said. "Get something from the Hotel Keeper. He must have something."

Horrible noises, like a chainsaw, like a truck changing gears, like a fire exploding, like a massive tree splitting in two, brought their conversation to an end.

The Hotel Keeper opened a wide cupboard of many shelves on which were large and small jars filled with seeds, leaves, grubs, bugs, bark, pods. Bottles containing green liquids of various hues filled other shelves.

"I have more than simply something," he said. "The trick is to ask me. This forest posseses a fantastic quantity of somethings that can cure or prevent what ails us. All to be lost when the forest is lost."

And he set to work. With mortar and pestle he ground six large seeds into a powder. With a tiny dipper he dripped a few drops of the darkest green liquid into the powder and mixed it in with a twig. Then he poured the mixture into a cup and presented it to her.

Like a child again, when a spoonful of medicine was a mystery to be solved by herself alone,

Beatrice obediently swallowed the mixture. Then she returned to her hammock and fell asleep. When she awoke, it was dawn again. She got up, put on her kimono, and again wrapped the woolen muffler around her neck.

"I suggest you leave the muffler," the Hotel Keeper said.

She left it and went out again into the forest, alone. Without asking herself if her throat was still hoarse, she began to sing. While the rainwater dripped from the leaves onto her lifted face, she sang as she had never sung before. And that was how she discovered she was healed. In the silence, after, she listened for Petrowski's answering song.

———

Ah! From deep in the forest, from high in the trees, *his* voice, that unmistakable voice came soaring out. Nearer and nearer he came, singing all the way. The beating of his wings was heard as he circled down. And then he was there, on a branch just above her! And how beautiful he

And then he was there

was, this bird whose whole body was pulsing with song. As the last note went gliding up and away, Petrowski flew down into Beatrice's arms, embracing her with wings whose span seemed even wider than she remembered.

C HOSEN FOR THEIR superior voices, Twenty-Seven Parrots flew into the train. Nervous, restless, they preened themselves rapidly and kept scratching their heads. When the train began to move, their fear sent up a small cloud of feathers.

"You'll forget your fear," Petrowski told them, walking up and down the aisle, "when you forget yourselves. You'll be singing to save not only *your* home but the home of every fellow creature in this forest. Please think about that enormous possibility."

With the help of the stewardesses the Twenty-

"You'll forget your fear when you forget yourselves."

Seven Parrots were guided into the plane bound for New York City. Mr. Alonzo had reserved enough seats and an extra one in case someone had counted wrong. Perched on the backs of their seats, the Parrots held fast as the plane rose. Among the passengers were several Brazilians, four Portuguese families, a French couple, a Spanish couple, a Japanese tour group, and a large Italian family.

When the Italian family began a conversation, the Parrots, familiar with the language of arias, burst into song, and when their song was over everyone applauded. Then one bold Parrot flew to a stewardess' shoulder and traveled up and down the aisle with her. The others flew among the passengers and spent the time learning songs in various languages. With all this attention the Parrots quickly adapted to being flown, a sensation quite different from flying on their own.

At the airport in New York City, Mr. Alonzo, with tears in his eyes, embraced Petrowski, kissing him on both cheeks. Several Parrots, af-

53

fected by this emotional reunion, flew up to Mr. Alonzo's head and shoulders or hovered above him.

A chartered bus took everyone to the hotel. The Twenty-Seven Parrots settled into the Diplomat Suite on the top floor. They looked down at the very tiny figures being rushed along like insects on a flood and darting in and out of openings at the bases of the high buildings. Fresh fruits and sunflower seeds and crackers and sparkling waters were brought to them all day long. With a modest-size orchestra they rehearsed their arias and became fast friends with the Musicians. Secretly, they imitated the musical instruments.

Very soon the day of their first public performance arrived. Clear skies, warm breezes. Central Park was packed to overflowing. The Mayor delivered the welcoming speech and, impatient for the show to start, the audience applauded before he could finish. And there in that great park, Petrowski and his Parrots sang so wonderfully they seemed to have been born singing together, and the Musicians seemed to have been born with their instruments in hand.

The pigeons and the crows and the varieties of other birds, and the mice and the rats, the cockroaches and the ants, all stopped worrying over where the next meal was to be found, and listened. The tumultuous applause at the end of the program swept the Twenty-Seven Parrots off their feet. Alarmed by what they mistook to be a fierce storm crashing down out of nowhere, they flew straight up in the air, wildly flapping their wings. But when they saw Petrowski and the Musicians bowing, the Parrots flew down and joined in.

WITH MR. ALONZO and Beatrice, and with Oliver and Lucia, Petrowski and his Parrot Troupe went on to other great cities. They sang in Hyde Park in London and in the Bois de Boulogne in Paris and in Tiananmen Square in China. After a performance in one vast square, people dug up the stones and planted trees, hoping to entice the Parrots to take up residence in that city. They sang in Australia, they sang in Africa.

Back in Brazil, thousands of messages came pouring into the presidential palace. By fax, by airmail, by e-mail, by telegrams, by telephone. Some were beseeching, some demanding. The messages came from everywhere in the wide world where Petrowski and his Parrots were singing. Forty more assistants were hired to handle this kind of deluge. President Fado's hair was fast turning white. He found himself in the coils of a dilemma, just as Petrowski had that fateful day on the train.

Estrella implored him to save Brazil from disgrace. "You must decree that no further harm is done to the forest."

"That I cannot do," he said. "You must try to understand, my dear, that we must sell to the world everything the world can possibly use. The Cattle Ranchers must clear more land for their cattle to graze, the Timber Merchants must cut more timber, the Oil Merchants must bring forth the oil that's under those trees. Everyone who wants that forest for whatever they want to do with it will boot me out of office. You, my dear, may have to go back to singing in that little cabaret."

57

"Read some of the messages, if not all," she pleaded.

"Are you suggesting that I save the forest a little at a time?" he asked.

"A little at a time won't do," she said. "That's the way we learn to play the piano or speak a foreign language. In this case, the little you save can't possibly keep up with the large that you'll lose. With no larger forest around to protect and nurture them, the little patches will be at the mercy of storms and pests. They'll be like orphans."

Unable to choose between the loss of the rainforest and the loss of the presidency, President Fado was unable to sleep at night. Days, he was unable to put his mind to any other matter. He was even unable to sign his name to the usual documents of little importance.

A T THE FOOT OF A very high
and craggy Himalayan mountain,
sad partings took place. Beatrice
yearned to return to the stages of Europe and
America and sing again for the thousands who
adored her. Lucia missed her mother and the
cathedral where she was baptized. Oliver complained of an allergy to more feathers than those
on one bird. The Musicians also chose to return
home. They said they could not risk their precious instruments to the care of the Yaks, the
shaggy oxen who were to carry everybody up the
steep trail. Neither could they understand, they

said, why Petrowski wished to sing at so great a height and to so few people.

"No big city up there," they said.

"Ah, but we shall be closer to the sky," said Petrowski.

On the backs of twelve Yaks, only Petrowski and Mr. Alonzo and the Twenty-Seven Parrots ascended the narrow, twisting, rocky trail.

"Yaks are shaggy because the air up high is cold and thin," Mr. Alonzo pointed out. "As we climb, simply remind yourselves to breathe calmly. Stay calm and you'll be fine."

Several of the parrots complained they were already having trouble breathing.

Petrowski, riding on the Yak at the head of the line, called back, "Save your breath!"

A Temple, way up on the edge of a precipice, was the first thing they saw as they neared the highest village in the world. Under the radiant sunset sky the Temple roof appeared to be solid gold. Way up on the Temple's many balconies, small figures clad in simple red and yellow garments, their heads smooth and brown, walked about.

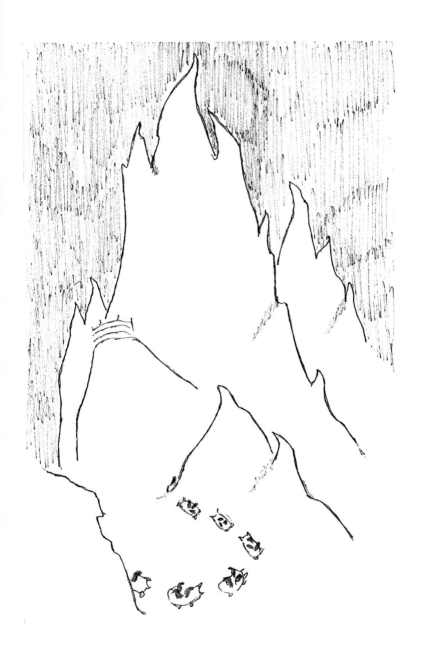

They ascended the narrow, twisting trail

The Parrots agreed among themselves that the figures were canaries, settling into their elaborate birdhouse for the night.

"They are not canaries," said Mr. Alonzo. "They are Monks. There are Christian Monks, as Lucia will tell you, and there are Buddhist Monks, and there are also other kinds. They all spend their lives being extremely religious."

Night was falling. Darkness was filling up the vast stony depths through which they'd climbed. In the high air the Villagers also seemed to be birds. From far they were tiny and quick, and their coats, boots, caps were of many vivid colors. But up close they were certainly people. The Villagers they passed in the narrow streets placed their palms together near their hearts and bowed from the waist. The Parrots tried the same greeting with their wings.

At the Temple gate, a Monk was waiting for them. "Please spend the night with us," he said, bowing.

The twelve Yaks carrying Petrowski, Mr. Alonzo, and the Twenty-Seven Parrots, filed in. They all settled down on thick cotton mats to sleep. The night was cold, and the Parrots crowded in among the shaggy Yaks for warmth.

"This temple is so close to the edge, it seems to be floating on air," Petrowski whispered to Mr. Alonzo. "Can it be?"

Then they both drifted off to sleep.

BELLS WAKENED THEM at dawn. Bells were ringing everywhere in the Temple, in every one of the countless chambers, lightly, as though tapped by the morning air.

"I wonder," said Mr. Alonzo, "if air sounds like bells in all the little air chambers of our lungs."

Several Monks, bowing, served them a breakfast of yak butter tea and *tsampa,* a barley dough that the Monks rolled in their fingers and the Parrots found delicious. When they had eaten, they were invited to visit the Lama, the wisest and oldest of all who dwelled in the Temple. The young Monk who was guiding them down the halls told them that nobody knew how old the Lama was because he refused to fragment Time into centuries and years and months and days. That only confuses things, the Lama said. The guess was that he was two hundred and seventy years old.

Following the Monk along endless halls, they passed open doors to chambers where more Monks were sitting in rows on the floor. Unmoving, they sat on small cushions and their hands were clasped serenely in their laps.

"They still look like birds to me," said the most contrary Parrot. "They're hatching eggs."

The Lama, too, was sitting on a cushion. Though he could be as old as the young Monks figured he was, his round, smooth face was a sweet child's face. The paintings on the walls of his chamber were of richly colored flowers and golden animals and birds.

The Lama on his cushion bowed to them and they all bowed to the Lama.

The Lama spoke. "It comes as no surprise to us," he said, "that parrots sing as grandly as do human beings. Goats sing, bears and wolves sing,

65

antelopes and elephants sing, spiders and bee-
tles sing, every creature sings. To breathe is to
sing. From our first breath to our last we are
singing our gratefulness for life."

Petrowski and all of the Parrots nodded
humbly. Mr. Alonzo, however, wanted more time
to think about it. Singing, he knew from long experience, required so much more than simply
breathing, and he also knew that any aspirant
who thought otherwise was never going to make
it. But his ears and his heart were listening close-
ly. The Lama just might be on the right path.

"Where are you from?" he asked.

"We are from the great Amazon rainforest,"
said Petrowski.

"Up here in the Himalayas," said the Lama, "the
air we breathe arrives from way down there. Oh,
there are other rainforests in other parts of the
world, but yours supplies the world with more
than any other. What do you hope to accomplish
with your tour?"

"We hope to save our rainforest from its destroyers," Petrowski replied.

"All living beings on this earth are grateful to you."

"You hope to save the air?" asked the Lama.

Mr. Alonzo's heart leapt for joy.

"The air," said Petrowski.

"Of course, the air," said the Lama. "All living beings on this earth are grateful to you and your followers for this tour. The number of lives you may save is beyond the counting. Tell me, when will you return to your origins?"

"After other countries, other cities," said Petrowski.

"If I may," said the Lama, "I suggest you return at once. Time is of the essence."

"And approach President Fado?" Petrowski asked.

"Whoever appears to be in charge," said the Lama.

"He may not grant us an audience," said Petrowski.

"Gather in his antechamber anyway," said the Lama. "Sit yourselves down on the floor or perch wherever you can. Say nothing, simply breathe. Eventually he will get the point."

The Lama bowed again, palms together, and said no more.

Flying from roof to roof, Petrowski and his Parrots sang for the Villagers who followed them along the winding streets. From the tops of the snowbound mountains ringing the village, the winds were flinging out snow banners, miles long, reminding Petrowski of the colored banners floating from that opera house where he first stepped out upon a stage.

O N A JET PLANE they flew to Brazil. They crowded into the antechamber of the presidential palace.

"What a test of courage this will be for President Fado," Mr. Alonzo said, speaking low to Petrowski.

Petrowski also spoke low. "If he refuses to grant us an audience, then exactly at eight o'clock, curtain time, we shall burst into song and our voices will fling open that door to his chambers."

The day wore on. Morning came and went and so did the afternoon, and in all that time

President Fado could not bring himself to invite Petrowski and his Parrots into his chambers. And because they were so quiet, he chose to believe they were not there at all. He was not used to this kind of behavior. The usual applicants for his attention were often offensively noisy. All he could do all day was drink cup after cup of coffee, black, each with several teaspoons of sugar.

When the evening began to deepen into night, Estrella slipped into his chambers.

Flashing a smile just like the one she wore when they first met eyes in that little cabaret, she said, "My dear, I have an idea. Deep in the rainforest is an old, really ancient, falling down opera house. The broad Amazon River at its front door, the dense jungle at its back. It was built, you recall, by rubber barons who wished to hear their favorite singers while they hauled away their riches. Give that opera house to Petrowski."

"An excellent idea," the President said. "An opera house to call his own. I've observed that when a man is profusely flattered, he grows fat and contented almost at once. Parrots are no different, I imagine. Petrowski will spend the rest of his life strutting around on that creaky stage, singing to the rats and the lizards."

"It's only an idea," she said.

Upstairs in her chambers, Estrella opened the large trunk filled with the costumes she had worn on those nights in the little cabaret. Spanish shawls with red roses and long silken fringes, silvery dresses, capelets trimmed with gold braid. Under the costumes lay the large key to the opera house. She had hidden the key as she had hidden her hopes to someday step out on a real stage, a golden curtain parting for her, and an orchestra at her feet.

Holding the key high, she ran down the stairs. The Minister of Culture, the General, and three Elder Statesmen were summoned. They arrived in a hurry, buttoning up their coats, pinning on their medals. Estrella got into an elegant gown, the President got into his swallow-tail coat, and with her help pinned all his

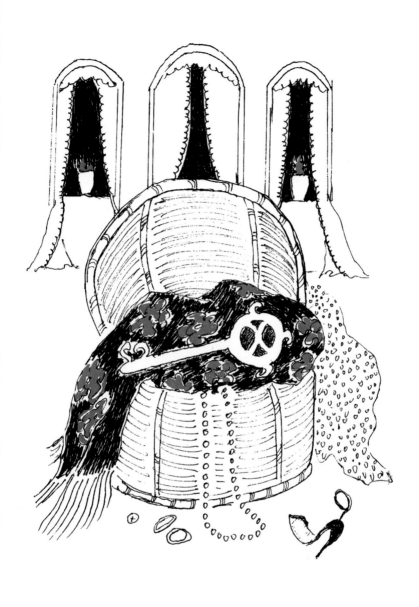

Under the costumes lay the large key to the opera house

beribboned medals on his chest. Then the door to the antechamber was thrown open.

It was exactly one minute before eight o'clock.

Several impatient Parrots flew in before the others and found perches for themselves on the chandeliers and vases and the ornate gold frames around the portraits of past presidents. One perched on the General's epaulet and was rudely shrugged off. Petrowski and Mr. Alonzo walked in together.

"My dear Petrowski," President Fado began. "This is the key to your very own magnificent opera house. Marble floors from Italy, curtains of French tapestry, seats of velvet from Portugal. And where is it, you ask? It is situated in your own eternal rainforest, no doubt near the very tree where you first opened your beak, a nestling."

With the key across both palms, he bowed to Petrowski.

"If you please," said Petrowski, "give the key to Mr. Alonzo. It was he who discovered me."

President Fado did as he was told and laid they key across Mr. Alonzo's palms.

Then Petrowski spoke. "This gift is not for myself alone. Singers of every kind and from everywhere will join us and the whole world will be listening. The Destroyers won't dare to blast or drill or saw or dig anymore. They'll douse their fires and retreat. Then everyone in the world will thank you for this great gift."

Shaken by Petrowski's prophetic words, the President was unable to utter further words of his own. So everyone withdrew and left him to his thoughts.

Alone, he threw himself down on the sofa. What had he done? Suppose that opera house became so precious to the world that the Destroyers would be forced to drop everything. What then? Why then they'd batter down the palace doors and send him into exile. He'd become like a homeless parrot himself, buffeted by foreign winds, with no familiar branch for the sole of his foot. Or suppose, instead, the Destroyers battered down that opera house just

as Petrowski was opening his beak to sing. Curiously, that thought was even sadder than the one about himself.

From out of the night Petrowski's voice came soaring into the palace. Like the air itself it filled every room, every niche, even lifting the ribbons on the President's troubled chest. Lifting him from the sofa, it wafted him lightly, like walking on air, to the window.

A curtain of clouds was lifting and the whole sky was a stage. Flying high above the city, the Great Petrowski and his Parrots were circling and singing. Entranced, all the city dwellers were pouring out their doors, leaning out their windows, gazing up at all those birds spiraling around among the stars.

The Great Petrowski and his
Parrots were circling and singing

Author's Note

HIGHFLYING THANKS to that Parrot in the open window in Cuernavaca, Mexico, who sang opera so beautifully, and to Julie and Leonardo, who always kept Petrowski's seedbowl filled to overflowing, and to Luanne Paul King, mezzo-soprano, who can fly a plane and feel like a bird, and to Judith Peck, opera lover, who also dwelled in the Brazilian rainforest, and to Bill Barich, far-ranging writer, who finds heroes in all species, and to Ann-Jeanette Campbell, editor, New York City, who fell in love with Petrowski, and to that little boy in the market whose T-shirt told the world of his promise to save the Amazon rainforest.

G.B.

GINA BERRIAULT lived most of her life in Northern California and published several novels including *The Son, Afterwards* (first published as *The Conference of Victims*), and *The Lights of Earth*. Her collected stories, *Women in Their Beds* won the National Books Critics Circle Award, the PEN/Faulkner Award, and the Rea Award for the Short Story. *The Great Petrowski* was completed in 1999.

———

Quod est praeclarum durat